McTAVISH
TAKES THE CAKE

Meg Rosoff

CANDLEWICK PRESS

Text copyright © 2019 by Meg Rosoff
Original illustrational style and cover art copyright © 2019 by Grace Easton
Interior illustrations by copy artist David Shephard,
based on and in the style of Grace Easton

First US edition 2021
First published by Barrington Stoke, Ltd. (Great Britain), 2019

Library of Congress Catalog Card Number pending
ISBN 978-1-5362-1375-1

21 22 23 24 25 26 LBM 10 9 8 7 6 5 4 3 2 1

Printed in Melrose Park, IL, USA

This book was typeset in Lora.

Candlewick Press
99 Dover Street
Somerville, Massachusetts 02144

www.candlewick.com

For Alex

CONTENTS

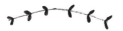

1

THE PEACHEYS COOK

"What's for dinner?" asked Ollie.

"Whose turn is it to cook?" asked Ava.

Betty stuck her head out of the kitchen.

"It's mine," she said. "On the menu tonight is vegetarian lasagna with a salad of baby greens, and for dessert, caramel-chocolate tart with cream."

"Great," said Ollie.

"Yum," said Ava.

Ever since Ma Peachey had decided that mothers should not be responsible for all the daily chores of family life, the Peachey children had taken over their share of the cooking.

They learned that making a meal wasn't difficult. You didn't have to be old and experienced to make lasagna or chocolate brownies. You didn't have to be married or very clever to roast a chicken or make fruit crumble. You just had to be able to read a recipe, measure ingredients, and follow directions.

In no time at all, the three Peachey children were making delicious meals. The Peachey family had never eaten so well.

Today was Wednesday, so it was Betty's turn to cook.

"I still have a great deal of work to do,"

Betty told Ava and Ollie, "so please go away."

Only McTavish was allowed to stay in the kitchen while Betty mixed flour into melted butter, then slowly added milk to make a sauce for the lasagna. McTavish paid close attention as she whisked together the oil, vinegar, mustard, and salt to make a dressing for the salad.

McTavish the rescue dog was often called upon to rescue the Peachey family. But in cases where rescue was not actually required, he still found ways to help.

While Betty was cooking, McTavish helped by cleaning up anything that fell on the floor. McTavish was faster and more effective than a vacuum, and although certain things (like lettuce) were not to his taste, he was excellent at cleaning up bits of cheese, cake, or bacon.

His services came in very handy when any of the Peachey children cooked. They were all very inventive when choosing recipes, but not always very tidy.

An average week might begin on Monday with Ava's roasted vegetable couscous followed by a special Moroccan milk pudding with rose syrup. Not to be outdone,

"It's toast," Ava said. "A little bit lik

only browner."

"Toast? You call this toast?

toast. Is it homemade? Wa

lovingly shaped by the hand

of our very own family? Wa

smooth and put in a warr

long as it needs? No, it

held the toast at arm'

dangerous. "This is

"Poison?" said

"This is n

"It is a cheap s

money-grubbing manu

care what real bread tastes like.

as well eat an old sponge."

Ollie stared at his father. Then at his toast.
Then at his father again. "It doesn't taste as
good as Betty's bread," he said, "but—"

Ollie would follow on Tuesday with roasted
chicken, mashed potatoes, and beans, with
crème brûlée for dessert. Betty always
cooked complicated vegetarian dishes on
Wednesday, while Ma Peachey preferred
a simple dinner of spicy tomato pasta with
fruit salad for Thursday. Pa Peachey was
supposed to cook on Friday, but he grumbled
about it so much that the rest of the family
just made sandwiches on Friday nights and
ate in front of the TV.

"I don't like to cook," Pa Peachey said.

"You like to eat," Betty observed.

"That's different," he said, which Betty
had to admit was true.

Cooking became so competitive in the
Peachey family that even breakfast was
exciting. Instead of a bowl of cereal, breakfast

Or o... had even s... every week, beca... much tastier toast. Whi... you'd eaten homemade sourdou... with butter and jam, it was difficult to ... anything else.

As week followed week, the Peacheys became more and more particular about their food. The problem with eating good, healthy, homemade food every day is that you don't really want to eat boring meals or junk food anymore.

So it happened that one fine morning, Pa Peachey sat down to breakfast, picked up a piece of toast from his plate, and gasped.

"What is this?" he demanded.

"I know what you're going to say," Pa Peachey said. "But any toast is not better than no toast. This so-called 'toast' is packed with chemicals, preservatives, and sugars, prepared in a fraction of the time it takes to make real bread, then packaged in plastic that is guaranteed to destroy the oceans."

Pa Peachey glared at his youngest child and pointed an accusing finger.

"You!" he said to Betty.

"Are you blaming Betty for the destruction of the oceans?" Ollie asked.

"My sourdough bread is still rising. It will not be ready till tonight," Betty explained.

"One day of supermarket bread will not kill us," Ava said.

"Perhaps," said Pa Peachey. "But this toast is fit only for a dog."

Everyone looked at McTavish, who

felt deeply offended. He thought Betty's sourdough bread was much better than supermarket bread.

"Betty is only nine years old," Ma Peachey said. "She has school and homework and friends and chores. It is a special treat for us when she makes sourdough bread. It is not her job."

"Why don't you make the bread yourself?" Betty asked Pa Peachey. "Then you could be certain of having it for breakfast every day."

"Maybe I will," Pa Peachey said with a thoughtful expression. "After all, if the youngest member of the family can make bread, it must not be very difficult."

Ollie and Ava turned to look at Betty.

Betty frowned.

McTavish blinked.

Ma Peachey looked nervous.

2

PA PEACHEY BAKES

The following morning was Saturday.

When Ma Peachey woke up, Pa Peachey was already hard at work in the kitchen.

Ma Peachey pulled on her clothes and started down the stairs. Before she reached the bottom, she heard a terrible noise.

BANG!

In the kitchen, she found Pa Peachey. At least she thought it was Pa Peachey. The person she thought was Pa Peachey was completely covered in flour. The floor was covered in flour. The counters were covered in flour. McTavish was covered in flour.

"Hello," said Ma Peachey.

"Hello," Pa Peachey said. "I'm afraid there has been an accident."

"I can see that," Ma Peachey said.

"The flour . . ." Pa Peachey said.

"Yes?" Ma Peachey said.

"Exploded."

Ma Peachey frowned. "Are you sure you didn't drop it? I have never heard of flour exploding before."

Pa Peachey shrugged. "There is always a first time. I have discovered that baking is a very dangerous pursuit. I might have been killed."

Ma Peachey did not ask how Pa Peachey might have been killed.

"And by the way, making bread is far more difficult than it looks," Pa Peachey told her.

"I can see that," said Ma Peachey.

"And far messier," Pa Peachey said.

"I can see that, too," Ma Peachey said. She went to the cupboard, took out a dustpan and brush, a bucket, a sponge, and an apron, and handed them to Pa Peachey.

"I have been thinking," Pa Peachey said, taking the bucket and putting on the apron. "Baking is a difficult and hazardous occupation. Betty is far too young to handle perilous tools such as knives and fire."

"And bags of flour?" Ma Peachey asked.

"Precisely," said Pa Peachey.

"But who will take over the bread baking?" Ma Peachey asked.

"I will," said Pa Peachey.

"I hope you will not find it too dangerous," Ma Peachey said.

"I have learned a few lessons from my first attempt," said Pa Peachey.

"Excellent," said Ma Peachey.

"Once I have cleaned up," Pa Peachey said, brushing the flour out of his eyes, "I will go to the store for more flour."

"Make sure to get the nonexploding type," Ma Peachey said.

"Ha, ha," said Pa Peachey.

McTavish followed Ma Peachey out of the kitchen, leaving a trail of white pawprints.

3

PA PEACHEY BAKES AGAIN

At noon that same day, Pa Peachey was still baking bread. He was still baking bread at two o'clock. And at three and at four and at six.

At seven o'clock that evening, Pa Peachey was still hard at work in the kitchen. No one dared disturb him to inquire about dinner.

At seven thirty, there was still no sign of dinner.

Ollie crept into the kitchen for some cheese and crackers, hoping Pa Peachey would not notice him.

But Pa Peachey did notice him.

"GET OUT! GET OUT! GET OUT!" Pa Peachey shouted.

Ma Peachey looked thoughtful. "I wonder if I should have a word with the chef," she said.

"Don't go near the kitchen if you value your life," Ollie said. "From now on, it is off-limits. Apparently."

"Pa Peachey is making bread," Betty said nervously.

"I know," said Ma Peachey, frowning. "A most interesting turn of events."

"You say interesting; I say disturbing," Betty said.

"You say disturbing; I say disastrous," Ollie said.

Ava said nothing, as she was just coming to a good part in A *History of Western Philosophy* by Bertrand Russell and wanted to know what happened next.

At approximately eight o'clock that evening, the aroma of baking bread emerged from the kitchen, making the poor hungry Peacheys feel even hungrier.

At approximately eight twenty-two, Pa Peachey stuck his head out of the kitchen and called the family in. "Ta-da!" he said, indicating his first-ever completed loaf of bread with a flourish. "I think you will find that this is the finest and most delicious loaf of bread ever made."

"It certainly looks good," Betty said.

Pa Peachey produced a large bread knife and attempted to cut a slice off the hot loaf. He sawed and he sawed, but the loaf of bread was too hard.

"This knife is woefully dull," Pa Peachey said with a frown.

Ollie disappeared into the garage and returned with a hacksaw. "This might work," he said.

HACK, HACK, HACK went Ollie's hacksaw. Then once more, HACK, HACK, HACK. After many minutes and much hard work, Ollie had managed to cut a slice of Pa Peachey's bread for each of them.

Pa Peachey's bread was hot. It looked good. It smelled good. But it was very chewy. You might even say it was as chewy as a shoe. Pa Peachey's bread was so chewy, in fact, that it was almost more like punishment than bread.

The Peachey family chewed and chewed. They chewed and chewed and chewed some more.

Time passed.

Betty sneaked half of her bread to McTavish, who took it to the corner, where he lay growling and tearing at it with his powerful teeth. But even McTavish could not chew Pa Peachey's bread. In the end, he managed to bite off a small piece and left the rest on the floor.

Maybe some rats will find it and take it away, McTavish thought.

When at last everyone had finished chewing, nobody asked for another slice. For one thing, their jaws were too tired to speak.

Ollie managed to mumble something through exhausted lips. "Is there anything else for dinner?"

Everyone looked at Pa Peachey, who only smiled happily.

"I think I have found my calling," he said. "Baking is both stimulating to the mind and relaxing to the spirit. From now on, you children can make the meals, but I will do all the baking."

At this, McTavish pricked up his ears.

It is worth remembering that dogs have very sensitive ears. They can hear sounds from four times the distance and at far higher frequencies than humans can.

Just now, McTavish could hear a kind of alarm bell ringing. Of course it is possible that he just imagined he could hear an alarm bell ringing, but it didn't really matter.

The idea of Pa Peachey as head baker sounded very alarming to McTavish.

4

PA PEACHEY BAKES SOME MORE

Pa Peachey did not make bread during the week. He was far too busy and tired after a long day at work. But on weekends, he rolled up his sleeves, put on his apron, closed the door to the kitchen, and baked. He baked and he baked and he baked.

Sadly, Pa Peachey was not very good at baking.

Most of what he made came out wrong. Not just a little bit wrong, but spectacularly, outstandingly wrong.

His sourdough bread was so heavy it could be used as a ship's anchor.

He tried baking cakes instead.

Instead of being light and delicate, his cakes were as heavy and flat as manhole covers. Instead of rising, they fell.

He tried other recipes.

Instead of tasting sweet, his cupcakes tasted strangely like liver. His fudge never hardened. His cookies turned to charcoal.

This was good news for McTavish, who was always willing to dispose of Pa Peachey's mistakes. Misshapen pies, wobbly tarts, burned cookies—McTavish selflessly devoured them all. He particularly liked the cupcakes that tasted like liver.

McTavish had cakes for breakfast, tarts for snacks, and cookies for supper. This was not a healthy diet for a dog, but McTavish felt that he owed it to the Peachey family to rescue them from the terrible baking. Which often did not taste as bad as it looked.

Weeks passed. Much to everyone's surprise, Pa Peachey's baking did not improve with practice.

"This is perfectly awful," Ollie said, spitting out an apricot tart that tasted like sand.

"I'd definitely eat this if I were starving to death," Ava said of salted toffee torte that could only be broken with a hammer.

"I wonder how he did this," Ma Peachey said, staring at a chocolate cake that looked like a deflated football.

"Practice makes perfect," Pa Peachey said cheerfully. "Now please give me space. I have work to do."

Practice did not make perfect for Pa Peachey.

He taught himself decorative icing and made piped roses that looked like toads.

His raspberry-and-lemon cheesecake weighed as much as an anvil.

His meringues pulled everyone's fillings out.

His brownies were black.

His sponge cake tasted exactly like a sponge.

McTavish continued to chomp his way through every failed dessert with courage and stamina. He was a very brave and steadfast dog.

Day after day, he dined on cake. Day after day, his waistline expanded. He became stocky, plump, and finally, he became almost fat. He was slow to leap out of bed in the morning, and most of the time he felt quite unwell.

"Do you mean to say you don't like my toffee cream tart?" Pa Peachey asked

McTavish one night as he dumped his latest failed experiment into McTavish's bowl.

McTavish lay on his bed and groaned. He couldn't eat another thing.

"Well, doesn't it just figure?" Pa Peachey muttered. "I toil and toil over a hot stove only to be met by rejection and contempt. Not merely from my family but from man's best friend as well! There's gratitude for you."

"Poor McTavish," Betty said, patting him gently. "This diet cannot be good for you. I shall have to help you."

From then on, Betty helped McTavish by eating half the ruined cakes, half the ruined puddings, half the ruined cupcakes, and half the ruined cookies. Some tasted very good, and some tasted as bad as they looked. The ones that tasted like liver always went to McTavish.

But as much as Betty and McTavish liked eating cake, and as much as they were willing to make sacrifices for their family, it soon became clear that this could not go on. McTavish no longer felt healthy. He and Betty could no longer run and play ball without feeling out of breath.

As the Peacheys' official rescue dog, McTavish felt obliged to save them from Pa Peachey's terrible desserts. And from a future of idleness and obesity.

Which he was willing to do, as soon as his stomach stopped hurting.

5

THE COMPETITION

One fine day, Pa Peachey arrived home from work in a state of high excitement.

"Look what I found in the newspaper!" he called as he opened the front door.

The Peachey children ran to greet him.

"A baking competition will be held," Betty read from the front page, "to discover the town's best and most ambitious baker. Judging will take place on the first Sunday of the month at the town hall—"

"By the mayor herself!" Pa Peachey interrupted. "And look here!" He pointed to the bottom of the poster. "First prize: five hundred dollars, donated by the Fame and Fortune Flour Company."

"Wow," said Betty. "Five hundred dollars could pay for cooking lessons for the entire family!"

"Wow," said Ollie. "With five hundred dollars we could buy all our cakes from the very excellent bakery in town."

Pa Peachey glared at him. "That will not be necessary, Oliver. Not when you have a top-notch baker such as myself right here at home."

Nobody said a word.

"Are you planning to enter the competition, Pa?" Betty asked.

"Of course I am planning to enter the

competition," Pa Peachey said. "Not only am I planning to enter, I am planning to design and build a creation so difficult, so surprising, so impressive, that I will certainly win first prize."

Pa Peachey punched his fist in the air and did a little victory dance, which caused Ollie to roll his eyes and Ava to creep out of the kitchen.

"I will need the support of my loving family in this difficult and challenging task," Pa Peachey said, "in the form of perfect solitude and quiet. A talented chef such as myself needs space to think and create. Without the intruding rabble of family life."

"Intruding?" said Betty.

"Rabble?" said Ollie.

Talented? thought McTavish.

"I'm afraid you will now have to leave me

in peace, for I have a great deal of thinking to do before I will be able to collect my five hundred dollars," Pa Peachey said, shooing his family out of the kitchen.

They were not reluctant to go.

6

Pa Peachey's Dream

Pa Peachey's mind was not on his job. It was not on his family. It was not on world events. He lived only for the moments he could resume his preparations for the contest.

Betty, Ollie, and Ava realized that once Pa Peachey arrived home from work each day, there would be no access to the kitchen. So they hastily grabbed food, plates, and cutlery before their father appeared.

Meanwhile, the kitchen was quiet.

There was no smell of burning.

There were no cries for help.

The smoke alarm did not go off.

It was very quiet.

Too quiet.

"Has Pa given up the baking contest?" Ollie asked.

"Perhaps he is quietly waiting for inspiration," Ma Peachey said.

Ava said nothing. She was reading *Nausea* by Jean-Paul Sartre (a famous French philosopher) but said the title had nothing to do with Pa Peachey's baking.

On the fourth evening of silence, Ma Peachey knocked cautiously on the kitchen door.

"Yes?" Pa Peachey said.

"May we come in?" Ma Peachey asked.

"Interruptions, interruptions. Am I never to have a moment's peace?" Pa Peachey complained.

Ollie, Ava, Betty, and McTavish crowded into the kitchen behind Ma Peachey. They all stared at Pa Peachey.

He was hard at work on a great pile of drawings.

Betty was puzzled. "Have you given up baking, Pa?"

"Given up? Don't be ridiculous," said Pa Peachey. "I am preparing the plans for my Grand Masterpiece."

"Grand Masterpiece?" Betty asked, eyes wide.

"Grand Masterpiece?" Ollie asked, mouth open.

"What sort of Grand Masterpiece did you

have in mind?" Ma Peachey asked, sounding a bit nervous.

"Why, the Grand Masterpiece that will win the town baking competition, of course!" Pa Peachey pulled out a notebook full of sketches. The sketches looked like plans for a house. A very large and complicated house.

"What are these drawings?" Ava asked.

"If you must know," Pa Peachey said, "they are drawings of the Palace of Versailles. It is the finest building in France. Two thousand three hundred rooms, formal gardens, home to King Louis XIV, the Sun King . . . oh, the glory!" Pa Peachey's face shone with joy.

The rest of the Peacheys looked puzzled.

"And?" Ma Peachey asked. "What will you do with these sketches of the Palace of Versailles?"

"I plan to construct the entire Palace of Versailles, detail for detail, stone for stone"—Pa Peachey paused for dramatic effect—"in gingerbread."

Betty gasped, Ollie guffawed, Ava sat down hard on a chair, and McTavish made a strange choking noise.

"Gingerbread?" Ma Peachey had turned pale.

"Why?" asked Ava.

"It sounds quite . . . challenging," Betty said.

"It is!" Pa Peachey exclaimed.

Ma Peachey was silent for a moment. "Excuse me, children, but I would like to talk with your father alone," she said at last.

Ava, Ollie, Betty, and McTavish left the kitchen.

Ten minutes later, Ma Peachey emerged.

"Pa Peachey and I have spoken," she said. "We have come to an agreement. Pa Peachey will pursue his dream of constructing the Palace of Versailles in gingerbread, and we will turn over the kitchen to him until the day the competition is judged. This is Pa Peachey's dream, and we must help him achieve it."

"Must we?" asked Ollie. "What if his dream is the dream of a madman?"

Ma Peachey gave Ollie a warning look. "We will all encourage and help him as much as possible toward the fulfillment of his dream."

"Even if he's the world's worst baker?" Ollie asked.

"Nothing he has ever baked has come out right," Ava added. "Ever."

"The Palace of Versailles with two thousand three hundred rooms and formal gardens may prove somewhat challenging for a man of Pa's skills," Betty said.

In his bed under the stairs, McTavish dreamed that Pa Peachey had taken up a nice sensible hobby like table tennis.

Ma Peachey looked at her children and sighed. "There is no accounting for dreams," she said.

7

THE PALACE
OF VERSAILLES

Pa Peachey sketched and sketched. At last he emerged from the kitchen, waving a sheaf of papers.

"I've done it," he said. "I have planned every element for construction of the Palace of Versailles in gingerbread. It is a feat never before attempted in the entire history of baking."

"I wonder why," Ollie said.

Ma Peachey shot him a stern look.

"I made a gingerbread house once," Ava said. "It fell down."

"But it tasted good," Ollie said.

Pa Peachey ignored them. "This is not an easy task," he said. "But I am confident that once the necessary three thousand seven hundred eighty-four separate pieces have been baked and glued together, my palace will come together in a blaze of glory."

"Three thousand seven hundred and eighty-four pieces?" asked Ma Peachey.

McTavish looked worried.

"Exactly," Pa Peachey said. "Each small piece carefully shaped, measured, cut, and baked from gingerbread, glued with sugar glue, and decorated with icing. It's going to be magnificent."

Nobody spoke.

Betty had found Ma Peachey's phone and was staring at it. "Wikipedia says that the famous hall of mirrors at Versailles contains more than three hundred mirrors. And was lit by three thousand candles."

"I don't think your father is interested in mirrors and candles," Ma Peachey said quickly. "There's plenty to think about with all those windows and balconies . . ."

"And arches and fountains and marble columns," Ollie added, looking over Betty's shoulder at the palace.

"And curly gold gates," Ava said.

"Of course, I can't speak for your father," Ma Peachey said, "but I don't believe it will be necessary to construct every single detail. Many elements could merely be suggested in a creative way."

Pa Peachey nodded. "Exactly," he

said. "Now I am afraid you must all leave me in peace. You may enjoy standing around goggling, but I have a great deal of gingerbread to roll out and cut and shape and bake and glue together and then decorate."

"And only two weeks to do it," Ollie said, eyes wide.

The minute Pa Peachey began to bake his 3,784 gingerbread cookies for the Palace of Versailles, McTavish's bowl began to fill once more with rejections.

McTavish did not like gingerbread that was burned to charcoal. He did not like gingerbread that was tougher to chew than a bone. To be honest, he was not the world's number-one fan of gingerbread even when it was cooked perfectly.

After just a few days, Betty was also thoroughly sick of gingerbread.

McTavish stood up and waddled back to his bed, tail between his legs. He was no longer willing to rescue Pa Peachey by eating all his leftovers. All he craved was a nice meaty bone.

I didn't count on this sort of duty when I became a rescue dog, McTavish thought. *This is downright inhumane.*

Betty was tired of eating leftover gingerbread, too. *It was nice when it first started*, she thought, but now all she felt was sick.

Betty followed McTavish back to his bed.

"Poor McTavish," she said, stroking his head. And then, "Your stomach certainly has become quite large."

McTavish looked at Betty. Her stomach had also become quite large.

This diet is terrible for both of us, he thought. *Betty is a girl and I am a dog. Neither of us is a garbage can. From now on, we will eat no more leftovers. In addition, we will embark on a strict program of exercise.*

It was time for action.

8

PA PEACHEY HARD AT WORK

The day of the baking competition grew closer.

The tension in the Peachey household grew, too.

Pa Peachey had taken a week off work. Now he rose early each morning and went immediately to the kitchen, where 3,784 pieces of gingerbread were arranged in teetering stacks on the table, on the

counters, on chairs, on stools, in cupboards, and on every shelf.

It made eating breakfast tricky. It made getting a glass of water or making a cup of tea tricky. It made having a sandwich or a piece of toast impossible.

Ma Peachey called Ava, Ollie, and Betty together and asked them to be patient.

"I am not saying that Pa Peachey's dream is a sensible one," she said. "But nonetheless it is his dream. And there is only one more week until the contest judging. So we must all be patient for a little while longer."

"OK," said Ollie. "But what if the Palace of Versailles encourages Pa to enter more contests? What if his next project is a life-size model of the Eiffel Tower made out of marzipan? Or the Empire State Building made out of cheese?"

"I don't think—" began Ma Peachey.

"It's possible," Ava said.

Ma Peachey sighed. "I think we'll have to cross that bridge when we come to it."

"Don't mention bridges," Ollie warned. "Pa Peachey might decide to carve the Golden Gate Bridge out of a pumpkin."

"Well, yes . . ." Ma Peachey said. "But Pa Peachey is a man of vision. He has big dreams, and it is wrong to destroy another person's dreams."

"Never mind," Ollie said. "Pa Peachey is perfectly capable of destroying his own dreams."

McTavish appeared with his leash in his mouth and stood in front of Betty.

"Woof!" said McTavish. "WOOF!"

"I think McTavish needs a walk," Ma Peachey said.

Betty pulled on her jacket and clipped on McTavish's leash.

Once out of the house, he began to run.

McTavish was not a large dog, but he was a determined and stubborn one. When McTavish ran, you had to run with him.

Together, he and Betty ran to the park. In the park, they ran up hills and down hills. They ran around trees and chased squirrels. McTavish found a ball, which he and Betty played with until dark. After all their games and exercise, they returned home flushed and happy, feeling a little bit healthier than they had earlier in the day.

Pa Peachey had placed a stack of rejected gingerbread in McTavish's bowl, but both Betty and he ignored it.

9

THREE DAYS TO GO

Pa Peachey was hard at work finishing the Palace of Versailles. No one was allowed into the kitchen to observe his progress, so the Peacheys set up a sandwich bar in the dining room. They had all grown sick of sandwiches and sick of washing dishes in the bathtub, but Pa Peachey's dream had to be respected.

The signs, however, did not bode well.

The signs were:

1. Bangs and crashes.

2. Howls of outrage.

3. Cries of torment and despair.

Three days before the contest deadline, Betty gathered her courage and knocked on the kitchen door.

"May I come in, Pa?" she asked.

"Disaster, disaster, disaster!" cried a voice from within.

Betty pushed the door and stuck her head into the kitchen. "Pa?"

Pa Peachey was sitting in the kitchen with his head in his hands. Approximately two thousand pieces of the Palace of Versailles were still stacked on the table in front of him.

A great number of pieces had already been glued together with sugar glue, but, so far, any resemblance to the actual Palace of Versailles was difficult to see.

The walls tilted in a number of unexpected directions. The roof sagged. The balconies clung for dear life to the walls, occasionally dropping off altogether. Pa Peachey had not yet created the east and west wings of the building, nor had he cut out the windows. He had not yet begun to construct the curly gates or shape the elaborate gingerbread sculptures. What he had created so far resembled a large garage stomped on by cows rather than the most majestic building in France.

Betty stared at the palace. She began to say, *Really it's not so bad.* But stopped. Because, really, it was very bad indeed.

She began to say, *I'm sure you can fix it.* But stopped. Because she felt fairly certain it was impossible to fix.

She began to say, *Never mind, I am sure the*

judges won't notice any flaws. But stopped. Because Pa Peachey's palace was so flawed, so totally flawed, so 100 percent flawed that it would be impossible for anyone not to notice.

Instead, Betty took a deep breath. "Pa," she said, "you have three days left to finish your palace, and I feel certain that your creation will be a most interesting and unique entry. There is no doubt in my mind that the judges will be amazed."

Betty heard a strange snorting noise that might have been Ollie listening at the door, but she ignored it.

Pa Peachey lifted his head from his hands. He looked up at Betty. His face was covered with flour and bits of gingerbread. Small spatters of colored icing patterned his clothing and the walls.

"Thank you for those kind words, dear Betty. I only fear that I may run out of time before my dream is complete," he said. "And that it will not measure up to the glorious vision in my head." Pa Peachey paused for a moment. "But most of all, I am afraid of disappointing my family."

"You can only do your best and work your hardest," Betty said. "That is what you have always told us. You will not disappoint us whatever you do. We will love and admire you whether you win the prize or not."

"Thank you, Betty," Pa Peachey said. "You are a good girl, and I am proud to have you as my daughter."

There was a long pause.

"But I still intend to win first prize."

10

TWO DAYS TO GO

More crashing and banging came from the kitchen.

Betty and McTavish went to the park and did more dashing and jumping and running and leaping and playing ball.

The most surprising thing that Betty discovered about exercising with a dog was that it did not feel like exercise; it felt like fun. The second-most surprising thing she discovered was how very good McTavish was at catching a ball.

Once, she threw the ball so high it bounced off the top of a tree. But McTavish jumped up on a park bench, leaped in the air, and caught it. Another time she threw the ball so hard it flew all the way over a pond.

There is no way on earth that McTavish will catch that ball, thought Betty. *I have thrown it much too hard and much too far.*

But before she could finish her thought, she saw a flash of gold headed toward the pond. Could it be? Yes! It was McTavish, running so fast that his legs were a blur. McTavish came to the edge of the pond, leaped into the water without a second's pause, and began to swim.

McTavish swam even faster than he ran, scattering ducks in all directions. In no time

at all, he had crossed the pond, scrambled out the other side, glanced up into the air—and caught the ball.

Everybody in the park clapped and cheered to see McTavish perform his amazing feat.

"If only there were an Olympics for dogs," said one man.

"He would surely win," said a woman.

"What an amazing dog," said a little boy.

"I wish he was mine," said a little girl.

McTavish held the ball tightly in his mouth and shook the water out of his coat. He trotted back around the pond to where Betty stood, and dropped the ball at her feet.

Betty smiled and kissed McTavish, even though he was very wet and smelled like a pond.

"Good dog, McTavish," Betty said with pride. "You are a very clever dog indeed."

Meanwhile, back at the house, Pa Peachey was so tired from working on his masterpiece that he staggered up to his bedroom for a rest.

While Pa Peachey rested, Ma Peachey snuck into the kitchen and made a large, healthy meal for dinner. Everybody was grateful not to be eating sandwiches again, even Pa Peachey.

Over dinner that night, the Peachey family talked about McTavish's skill at catching balls, about German philosophy, and about the weather.

Nobody dared ask Pa Peachey how his project was going.

11

ONE DAY TO GO

Once again, Betty and McTavish were playing ball in the park.

Betty threw the ball as far as she possibly could. Then she and McTavish ran after it as fast as they possibly could.

Betty threw the ball as high as she possibly could, and she and McTavish leaped up in the air as high as they possibly could to catch it.

They played catch for some time.

After playing catch, Betty and McTavish ran all the way around the pond. They chased some geese. They dodged around trees and tried to tag each other. They ran up a hill and down a hill. Then up the hill again. By the time they went home, they were huffing and puffing. And happy.

"Are you and McTavish planning to run a marathon?" Ollie asked.

"We're getting back in shape after eating too many cakes," Betty said. "And it's working. Come on, Ollie, I'll race you upstairs."

But Ollie wasn't interested in racing, so she raced McTavish instead.

Ma Peachey came downstairs from her office.

Ollie was combing his hair in a new way that he hoped might attract more girlfriends, while Ava read *Philosophical Fragments*, a book by the Danish philosopher Søren Kierkegaard that no one has ever understood.

"Do you really understand that?" Ma Peachey asked Ava.

"Of course," Ava said, and went back to her reading.

Ma Peachey shrugged. "Has anyone seen your father?" she asked.

Ollie and Ava shook their heads.

"A bad sign," Ma Peachey said. "Has anyone heard your father?"

Ollie and Ava shook their heads.

"Another bad sign," Ma Peachey said. She sighed. "I think I had better investigate."

Ma Peachey carefully pushed open the kitchen door. Ava and Ollie followed close behind.

Inside, Pa Peachey was still at the kitchen table, his head resting on a pile of gingerbread. He was fast asleep, snoring softly.

"Oh dear," whispered Ma Peachey.

"Oh dear," Ava whispered.

Ollie looked at the Palace of Versailles.

"Oh dear," he whispered.

They all stared.

"Oh dear," they all whispered at once.

"Do you think we can fix it?" Ava whispered.

"No," Ollie whispered.

"I'm afraid your brother is right," Ma Peachey whispered. "I don't think anyone could fix it."

"Not NASA," whispered Ollie. "Or Michelangelo. Or Albert Einstein. Or . . . "

"We get your drift," whispered Ava.

Ma Peachey ushered them out of the kitchen.

"What on earth are we going to do?" she asked in a normal tone of voice.

Upstairs they could hear Betty and McTavish leaping and running and jumping. The ceiling rattled and shook.

"It's their new exercise program," Ollie explained. "And it's very annoying."

Ma Peachey put her hands over her ears. "I suppose we shall just have to wake Pa Peachey and let him try to finish his masterpiece."

"But he'll be a laughingstock!" Ollie said.

Ava picked up her book. "I am just now reading about the role of doubt and faith in human philosophy. And although doubt is important, faith is important, too. I think it might be best to hide our doubts and let Pa

Peachey know we have faith in him."

"But we don't," Ollie said.

Ma Peachey gave him a stern look. "We do," she said.

"Pa is certain to be awarded last place," Ollie said.

"There is no award for last place," Ava said. "There will be a winner and a second place, and maybe even a third. But everyone else will just be . . ."

"Losers," Ollie said.

"I think your sister is right," Ma Peachey said. "Short of a miracle, we must simply show that we have faith in your father."

"But what if we don't have faith?" Ollie said.

"Then we must pretend," said Ma Peachey.

Just then, McTavish and Betty thundered

down the stairs, panting and laughing. They flopped onto the floor and lay there.

"How is Pa's palace looking today?" Betty asked.

"How do you think?" Ollie asked.

"Oh," said Betty. She felt suddenly sad. "Pa Peachey is not very good at baking, but in the past he has been very good at being a kind and understanding father," she said to McTavish. "We must think of a way to help him. What on earth can we do?"

McTavish looked thoughtful. He was considering the same question.

He had rescued the Peachey family many times in the past. But could he rescue Pa Peachey from being the worst baker in the world?

This time he was not so sure.

12

THE BIG DAY

The morning of the judging arrived.

Despite Ollie hoping that the world might end a few hours before daybreak, it did not.

Despite Ollie hoping for a very dense fog that would reduce visibility to just a few inches, or a blizzard that would shut down all the roads and cause the competition to be canceled, it was a beautiful, clear, and sunny day.

Pa Peachey had worked all night, gluing

and decorating. In the final few hours, he threw his entire heart and soul into the project, every ounce of his determination and skill.

The Palace of Versailles looked terrible.

Pa Peachey was too tired to notice how it looked. But the rest of the Peacheys had resigned themselves to humiliation and ridicule. It was impossible to imagine any other result.

"Poor, poor Pa," Betty said.

"Poor, poor Pa," said Ava.

"Poor, poor us," said Ollie, hoping nobody he knew would be at the competition.

Ma Peachey shook her head sadly.

Everybody helped transfer the terrible Palace of Versailles onto a large wooden board. Ma Peachey wrapped it around and around with a loose cover of brown paper for protection. Then she and Ollie placed it ever so carefully into the trunk of the car.

The Peacheys all climbed into the car with infinite care so as not to joggle Pa's creation. Pa Peachey looked tired and dejected.

Ma Peachey drove slowly and carefully.

Pa Peachey was so tired from his all-night efforts that he kept nodding off on the way to the town hall.

When at last Ma Peachey stopped the car, he jerked up from a dream.

"First prize? Why, I am so honored! Thank you, Madam Mayor, and thank you, Fame and Fortune Flour Company! Five hundred dollars will allow me to achieve ever greater feats of baking!" Pa Peachey blinked happily, still half-asleep.

"Wake up, Pa." Ava shook his shoulder gently. "We've just arrived at the town hall. They haven't begun the judging yet."

"Oh," Pa Peachey said.

Betty and McTavish leaped out of the car and began running in figure eights around the parking lot.

"Wheeee!" Betty shouted.

"Woof!" McTavish answered.

Ma Peachey and Ollie removed the Grand Masterpiece from the trunk of the car.

"I'll take that," Pa Peachey said.

"I think it might be better if I carried it, Pa," Ollie said. "You look very tired."

Pa Peachey sighed. "I suppose I am tired. And I suppose if you carry the masterpiece, I can practice my speech."

Nobody asked which speech he was practicing, though everyone in the Peachey family had the same nervous idea—that Pa Peachey was practicing his victory speech.

Betty had brought McTavish's ball, and the two of them practiced throwing and catching.

"Settle down, Betty," Ma Peachey said.

Betty frowned. "But we need more exercise. McTavish and I are on the road to being fit and healthy."

"Yes," Ma Peachey said. "But perhaps now is not the right moment."

The Peacheys approached the town hall, walking sideways and carrying Pa's masterpiece with great care. Other contestants arrived with their masterpieces, some wrapped up and some not. The unwrapped entries caused Betty's heart to sink. They were professional, elegant, beautifully constructed and worthy of a five-hundred-dollar prize.

One was a cake in the shape of a cactus. The cactus was so lifelike you had to look carefully to see that it was not a genuine desert plant.

Another cake looked exactly like a Formula One race car.

There was a beautiful, shiny loaf of bread in the shape of a blue whale.

Every entry looked amazing. Except for Pa Peachey's.

A large handwritten sign directed entrants to a row of long tables set up on the lawn beside the town hall. A crowd had already gathered, and a banner read WELCOME, BAKERS, TO THE CONTEST and then underneath that, SPONSORED BY THE FAME AND FORTUNE FLOUR COMPANY.

Ma Peachey and Ollie sidestepped carefully in the direction of the long tables, dreading the moment when the brown paper would have to come off.

13

McTavish's Near Miss

After days of constant throwing and catching, McTavish and Betty were finding it impossible to stand still. So they had a hopping race from one side of the huge lawn to the other. McTavish was not a very good hopper, so he ran rings around Betty instead.

Ma Peachey and Ollie approached the long table, balancing Pa Peachey's masterpiece between them on the large board.

Betty and McTavish played catch.

Sometimes McTavish added a little twist in the air, just to show off. Sometimes he waited till the last moment to jump so that everyone gasped and thought, *He will never catch it this time.* But McTavish always, always caught the ball.

Even when Betty's throw wasn't very good, McTavish caught the ball.

Which made what happened next so very surprising.

Betty threw the ball high into the air.

McTavish looked up to judge where it was headed, then coiled his body up like a spring and leaped.

Afterward, nobody could quite agree on exactly what had gone wrong.

Perhaps McTavish forgot to calculate that extra bit of body fat he still carried around his middle.

Perhaps Betty's aim was the problem.

Perhaps there was a slight spin on the ball, which caused it to change direction in midair.

Perhaps a gust of wind blew it off course at the very last moment.

All the onlookers turned to watch as the ball flew above the crowd. All the onlookers watched as the ball flew directly toward McTavish's jaws. And all the onlookers gasped as the ball flew—not into McTavish's jaws but just barely, ever so slightly, beyond them.

McTavish snapped his mouth shut, but the ball kept going.

It flew up, up, up, and then, thanks to the miracle of gravity, it began to fall down, down, down. Instead of hitting the ground, the ball clipped the edge of the long table and ricocheted sideways at great speed.

Ollie watched with horror as the ball headed straight toward him.

It might be good to remember that it is a natural human reflex to duck when a ball is headed straight toward you at great speed.

Ollie ducked.

He did not let go of the board, but when he ducked, his side of the board dropped by approximately three feet. This meant that his side of Pa Peachey's masterpiece also dropped by approximately three feet.

A gasp went up from the crowd as the Palace of Versailles, still entirely covered in brown paper, began to slide.

But before Ollie could react to the sliding palace, McTavish's ball whacked him on the side of his head, causing him to shout "OW!" and fall sideways.

The Palace of Versailles began to slide off the board. Ollie put his hand out to stop it. But it was too late.

The gingerbread palace slid off the end of the board and plummeted to the ground. It met its end with a muffled noise that was somewhere between a crunch and a thud.

Pa Peachey's masterpiece lay in a terrible heap on the ground, still covered in brown paper.

14

Disaster for Pa Peachey

"NOOOOOOO!" cried Pa Peachey.

"NO!" cried Betty and Ava and Ollie and Ma Peachey together.

The judges and rival contestants all rushed to the scene of the disaster.

Pa Peachey dropped to his knees beside the large tangled pile of brown paper and broken gingerbread.

"My beautiful palace!" he cried.

McTavish was nowhere to be seen.

"My glorious palace!" Pa Peachey cried. "Oh, the tragedy! Oh, the heartache!"

It is an interesting fact that not one of the judges had seen Pa's palace before it was smashed to smithereens. When they saw it lying in a heap on the ground, it was easy to think it had once been a creation of exquisite beauty. The judges covered their faces with their hands. They assumed sorrowful expressions. They circled Pa Peachey and his ruined palace, shaking their heads. They could only begin to imagine the amount of work that had gone into building the entire Palace of Versailles out of gingerbread.

"It must have been glorious," one of them said in a hushed voice.

"It must have been a work of art," another said, nearly choking with sorrow.

"It must have been unlike anything we've ever seen," another said, holding back actual tears.

"You can say that again," Ollie muttered.

Somebody handed Pa Peachey a dustpan and brush.

Sadly, and with great dignity, Pa Peachey began to sweep up the remnants of his broken dreams.

15

FLOUR FOR LIFE

Pa Peachey did not win the five-hundred-dollar prize that day.

First prize went to a most amazing model of the *Titanic* made entirely of chocolate, sinking into the sea surrounded by marzipan lifeboats.

Second prize went to the beautiful blue whale made out of rye bread.

And third prize went to the cake that looked so much like a cactus nobody dared touch it for fear of getting pricked.

The Peachey family stayed through the award ceremony because only sore losers sneak off home when they have not won. They clapped when each winner was announced. But they all felt very downcast.

Pa Peachey looked like a man whose dream had been shattered in a terrible ball-throwing accident.

Which it had.

The Peachey family looked like a group of people who had been through a most distressing and emotional experience.

Which they had.

McTavish looked like a dog who had managed to save his family from disaster and humiliation without anyone even noticing.

Which he had.

Betty looked at her father. His sadness moved her to tears.

"Let's go home, Pa. There will be other contests," she said, taking his hand.

But just as they were about to set off for home, they heard the mayor call Pa Peachey's name.

"Will Mr. Peachey please come up to the stage to join the winners?"

A confused Pa Peachey made his way through the crowd and took his place onstage, where he looked this way and that, wondering what could possibly happen next.

The mayor handed Pa Peachey an envelope and shook his hand.

"Mr. Peachey," the mayor said, "in recognition of the extraordinary toil and creativity you invested in your entry, not to mention the unfortunate destruction of the magnificent Palace of Versailles, the Fame and Fortune Flour Company hereby awards you a consolation prize of a year's supply of free flour."

The crowd clapped and stamped and cheered and whistled. Pa Peachey turned bright red. The barest hint of a smile appeared on his haggard, exhausted face.

"Thank you," he said softly, and shook the mayor's hand. He was too overcome with emotion to say anything else.

After everyone had congratulated the winners and admired the cakes, Betty threw her arms around her father.

"Oh, Pa," she said, "I am more sorry than words can ever express that my ball caused your palace to crash to the ground."

"Never mind, Betty," Pa Peachey said

cheerily. "All's well that ends well. I am planning to use at least five hundred dollars' worth of flour this year. So my consolation prize has turned out to be nearly as good as winning. And," he said in a low voice, "I feel quite confident that my Palace of Versailles would have won first prize had it not been for the unfortunate accident."

The year's supply of free flour made Ma Peachey nervous.

"I think it is time to go home and celebrate today's triumph," she said, "and think about free flour at another time."

McTavish crept up behind Pa Peachey with his tail between his legs.

"Here is the hero—I mean, the villain—of the day," Ollie said. "If it weren't for the fact that you missed your ball and it whacked me in the head, McTavish, Pa Peachey's masterpiece would still be in one piece."

"Life is full of senseless tragedy," Pa Peachey said, shaking his head. "But after all, McTavish is only a dog. What else can we expect from him but foolish bungling?"

Only a dog? thought McTavish. *Foolish bungling?*

McTavish did not expect to receive credit for all the clever plans he made for the Peachey family, but it did sometimes hurt his feelings when they went so unnoticed.

But just then Ollie swept McTavish up in his arms.

"McTavish," Ollie whispered in his ear, "I don't know if you missed that ball by mistake or on purpose, but either way, you are the hero of the day, and we all know it." He glanced at Pa Peachey. "Almost all of us, that is."

Betty and Ava came and hugged him, too.

"You are the best dog in the entire world," Betty whispered.

"And the smartest," Ava said.

"I have no idea what we would do without McTavish," Ma Peachey added, patting him fondly on the head.

You'd be lost, McTavish thought.

But he was far too polite to say it out loud.